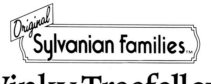

Winky Treefellow Builds a Kite

Simon Harwood

FANTAIL

ARISTOTLE and Arabella Treefellow have triplets, three sons who are called Winky, Blinky and Grumpy. It is very difficult to tell one from the other. In fact, the only way to tell them apart is to see what each one is doing. If one's reading a book, then it's Winky. The one who is asleep in the corner has to be Blinky. And the one who is always complaining is Grumpy.

Arabella finds it easier just to call them 'my boys' or 'my darlings'.

ARISTOTLE Treefellow is the teacher in Sylvania. He is very clever and spends all his time reading books when he is not teaching.

There are so many books in the Treefellows' house that it looks like a library. They have books on every possible subject, from Astronomy, the study of stars, to Zoology, the study of animals.

ONE day, Winky, who spends most days flicking through one book or another, came across 'K' for Kite in his father's Encyclopaedia Sylvania.

"A light frame covered with thin material, designed to be flown in the air at the end of a long string," Winky read out loud.

He then went on to read how kites could be made of anything as long as they were light. They could also be decorated with brightly coloured tails. Winky was fascinated.

THAT evening, Winky asked his father about kites.

"Yes, well, when I was a boy, I had a kite. Yellow, yes, it was a yellow kite. I made it with the help of Ernest Evergreen. Didn't fly though!" said Aristotle.

"It didn't fly?" asked Winky. "Why not?"

"Can't really remember. Ernest will know, in fact, now I think about it, he did get it to fly," pondered Aristotle.

"ERNEST, Ernest, are you there?" called Winky from outside Ernest Evergreen's workshop.

Winky jumped with fright as the window flew open.

"Sorry to startle you, it's just that I can't open the door at the moment," said Ernest, who had poked his head out of the window.

"That's alright," said Winky. "I came to ask you about kites."

"Ah, just a minute, I have my manual somewhere," said Ernest and with that he disappeared back into his workshop.

AFTER a lot of banging and crashing about, Ernest reappeared at the window with a dusty old book.

"Here you are Winky, everything you need to know about kites. I am sorry that I can't help you further. I'm working on a new invention. Do you know, it is so big that I can't get in or out of my workshop?" said Ernest.

After thanking Ernest, Winky set off home with the manual under his wing.

THAT afternoon, Winky read and re-read Ernest's manual.

"It's not that easy," thought Winky. "I'll have to get some help."

"I know, I'll go and see Logan. He sometimes helps Ernest, so maybe he'll help me," said a cheerful Winky.

But when Winky arrived at the Evergreen's house, he met Ashley and Preston who told him:

"Logan's working with Ernest on the new invention."

"But we'll help," said Preston.

THE three young builders spent the afternoon clearing a space in Preston's room. They collected wood from the garden shed, newspapers from under Forrest Evergreen's armchair and cloths from Honeysuckle Evergreen's rag basket.

"We just need some glue and string," said Winky. "Then we can start."

"Maybe we had better start tomorrow," said Ashley. "It's getting rather late."

ON the way home, Winky popped into Rocky Babble-brook's shop.

"Please may I buy some string and glue," shouted Winky, who was so small that he couldn't see over the shop counter.

Rocky smiled down at Winky and asked what he was up to.

"I am building a kite with Ashley and Preston," answered Winky.

"Well, in that case, you'll need a lot of string and only a little glue," stated Rocky.

ROCKY had to lend Winky his son's trolley to carry everything home.

"Bubba won't mind as long as you bring it back when you have finished with it," said Rocky as he closed the shop for the night and waved Winky off.

BRIGHT and early the following morning, Winky, Ashley and Preston set to work on their kite. By lunchtime, they had created something that certainly looked like a kite.

"There's more glue on you and Preston than on the kite," laughed Ashley.

"You can talk, look in the mirror," giggled Winky.

Ashley was covered in black marks from the newspapers.

"We'd better clean up a bit before we try out the kite," said Ashley.

IT was a beautiful day as the three kite builders walked to the top of a small hill close to the Evergreen's house.

"Well, according to the manual, one of us has to hold the kite up in the air while the other runs away letting the string out slowly," explained Winky.

They tried and tried but the kite just crashed to the ground each time. After about an hour, they were tired out and tangled in string.

AS the three lay on the hill catching their breath, what looked like a large brightly coloured sun appeared over the top of the trees. Under this large round object hung a basket and in the basket stood Ernest and Logan.

"Hello," called Logan. "How do you like our new invention? It's a hot air balloon."

"At least it works," called back Winky, "which is more than can be said for our kite!"

Ernest explained from his basket that they needed a strong wind to fly the kite.

ERNEST had an idea! He brought the hot air balloon down onto the hill.

"If you give me the kite and let out the string slowly, I'll take the kite up to the wind," he explained.

As the balloon climbed back into the sky, Winky, Ashley and Preston held on to the string, letting it out a bit at a time.

"Ready," called down Ernest. "Here we go."

With that, he released the kite.

THE wind caught the kite and it danced and climbed higher and higher.

Winky jumped for joy, the others laughed and cheered.

"It works, our kite is flying!" shouted Winky.

Ernest turned to Logan and said:

"It's been a good day for building and flying. But now it's time for tea."

FANTAIL PUBLISHING, AN IMPRINT OF PUFFIN ENTERPRISES
Published by the Penguin Group
27 Wrights Lane, London W8 5TZ, England
Viking Penguin Inc., 40 West 23rd Street, New York, NY 10010, USA
Penguin Books Australia Ltd, Ringwood, Victoria, Australia
Penguin Books Canada Ltd, 2801 John Street, Markham, Ontario, Canada L3R 1B4
Penguin Books (NZ) Ltd, 182-190 Wairau Road, Auckland 10, New Zealand
Penguin Books Ltd, Registered Offices: Harmondsworth, Middlesex, England

First published by Fantail Publishing, 1989
13579108642
Copyright © 1989 Epoch Co Ltd
All rights reserved

014 0900136

Made and printed in Great Britain by
William Clowes Limited
Beccles and London